Reading Es in S

GOVERNING THE WORLD

ANCIENT GOVERNMENTS

Nancy Shniderman

Perfection Learning®

To Jeff

EDITORIAL DIRECTOR: Susan C. Thies

EDITOR: Judith A. Bates

COVER DESIGN: Michael A. Aspengren

INSIDE DESIGN: Mark Hagenberg

PHOTO RESEARCH: Lisa Lorimor

IMAGE CREDITS

Northwind Picture Archives: pp. 6–7, 8 (top), 9, 10, 13, 14, 16, 17, 18–19, 29, 38, 42; © Snark / Art Resource: p. 31

ArtToday: pp. 12, 15, 28 (top), 32, 44, 45; Corel: cover, back cover, pp. 3, 4–5, 8 (bottom), 20, 21, 22, 23, 24–25, 26, 27, 28 (bottom), 33, 34, 35, 36–37, 37, 39, 40, 41, 43, 46, 47, 48

1 2 3 4 5 BA 06 05 04 03 02

Paperback ISBN 0-7891-5889-2

Table of Contents

Mayan ruins in Copan, Honduras

Introduction

People probably have lived on Earth for around two million years. **Archaeologists** explore the ruins where early humans lived. They examine tools and fossils these humans left behind. They even study skeletons of **prehistoric** people. These **artifacts** give scientists an idea of when and how early people lived.

The ages of the artifacts are estimates. The time periods in which they originated are not exact. Artifacts usually are calculated to be "around" a certain date.

Archaeologists have learned that prehistoric people lived in family groups, or clans. One member, usually male, controlled the clan. Eventually, family groups merged with other family groups. The wisest or strongest was the group leader.

Early humans were hunters and gatherers. They were **nomads** who roamed in search of food. They gathered, or collected, plants that grew wild—fruit, berries, grain, and herbs.

THE DEVELOPMENT OF AGRICULTURE

Agriculture developed around 9000 B.C. This changed human lifestyles. People learned to farm, so they no longer needed to search for food.

More people began living in one place. The larger clans merged into tribes, and the tribes formed villages. A way to organize large groups of people became necessary. This led to ancient governments.

THE DEVELOPMENT OF WRITING

Around 3500 B.C., people invented early forms of writing. They drew pictures on the walls of caves and carved pictures on stone pillars, walls, or tablets. They invented symbols that stood for ideas or words.

Two of the earliest forms of writing were cuneiform and hieroglyphics. Cuneiform used symbols. Hieroglyphics was a form of picture writing.

Writing allowed humans to document their activities. This ended the prehistoric period in human history. Civilizations began recording information about their communities. They wrote down laws of their governments.

THE DEVELOPMENT OF INDEPENDENT CIVILIZATIONS

Early civilizations had little contact with one another. They developed independently. They did not exchange ideas or knowledge. Much of their progress depended on the natural resources around them. Civilizations usually began near water sources.

Egyptian Hieroglyphics
The ancient Egyptians used about 700 hieroglyphic symbols, including 24 signs for single sounds. Hieroglyphics can be read from top to bottom and right to left.

Historians date the first civilizations back to when they left written records. Four independent civilizations began around 3500 B.C. They started in the Fertile Crescent, the Nile Valley, the Indus River Valley, and the Huang He Valley. During the ancient era, civilizations were also found in Europe, Africa, Japan, and the Americas.

SOME FORMS OF ANCIENT GOVERNMENTS

There were several common forms of ancient governments.

Democracy

Democracies are governments ruled by many. This form of government was created in the Greek **city-state** of Athens. Generally, qualified citizens participate in the government by attending **general assemblies** and by voting. Democracies were uncommon in ancient civilizations.

Democracies are different today. Citizens are indirectly involved in governmental decisions made through their elected representatives. Forms of democracies are popular all over the world. The United States has the oldest democracy in the modern world.

Monarchy

A monarchy is a form of government in which one person rules. A monarch has the right to rule during his or her lifetime. The heirs of monarchs inherit that right. A series of rulers from the same family is often called a *dynasty*.

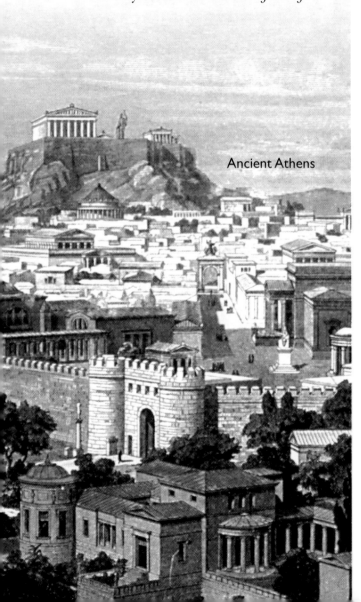

Ancient Athens

Monarchs include kings, queens, emperors, and empresses. A monarch might also be a prince. Kings in Egypt were called *pharaohs*.

In earlier times, the power of a monarch was **absolute**. It was thought that the ruler only had to answer to his or her god.

Monarchs always lived in far more luxury than their subjects. They had more privileges and rights. So when monarchs ruled, their subjects often thought they were treated unfairly.

Some monarchies still exist today, but in different forms. England is an example of a monarchy blended with a democracy.

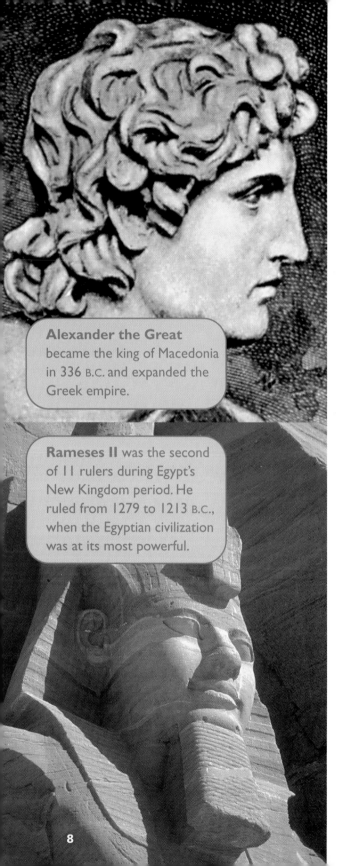

Alexander the Great became the king of Macedonia in 336 B.C. and expanded the Greek empire.

Rameses II was the second of 11 rulers during Egypt's New Kingdom period. He ruled from 1279 to 1213 B.C., when the Egyptian civilization was at its most powerful.

Oligarchy

An oligarchy is a government controlled by a limited number of people. These rulers shape laws and policy in order to gain personal wealth. They care little for the general public.

Most early Greek city-states had oligarchies.

Republic

A republic usually refers to a form of government in which ultimate political power comes from the people. Citizens elect representatives to manage the government. This is also known as a representative or indirect democracy. The United States is a representative democracy.

Theocracy

Theocracy is a "government by god." A religious group or person claims the power to rule. Rulers are considered representatives of their gods. They believe that they have a divine right to rule, saying that their god appointed them through their ancestors.

In ancient times, kings or queens headed such governments. Often these rulers were also priests or priestesses. These governments were both monarchies and theocracies.

Tyranny

Tyranny is a government where one powerful person rules. Tyrants do not come into power because of family ties or by being elected. Tyrants are **aristocrats** who usually seize power by force. These rulers make promises, such as to lower taxes, that appeal to lower classes. Then poorer people support tyrants and place them in power. Other aristocrats resent tyrants because of these promises.

In early governments, tyrants had absolute powers. They were strong rulers. Many Greek tyrants were kind, capable rulers. But others were often cruel.

END OF THE ANCIENT WORLD

The ancient Roman Empire collapsed in 476 A.D. That marked the end of the ancient world.

The historical period called the Middle Ages began around 500 A.D. Monarchies and **feudal** governments replaced ancient forms of government.

The Karnak Temple built for Rameses III of Egypt was nearly 200 feet long. The court is surrounded by statues of Rameses III.

CHAPTER 1

The Fertile Crescent

M any historians believe that civilization began in the Fertile Crescent. This area had rich soil and was shaped like a half-moon, or crescent. The Fertile Crescent began along the eastern shore of the Mediterranean Sea. It stretched to the Persian Gulf. This region of southwest Asia is present-day Iraq.

THE SUMERIANS

The eastern section of the Fertile Crescent was Mesopotamia. *Mesopotamia* is a Greek word meaning "between the rivers." The Tigris and Euphrates Rivers border the region. These two rivers empty into the Persian Gulf.

Sumerians were one of the first people known to live in the Fertile Crescent. The Sumer civilization began around 3500 B.C. It lasted until around 2000 B.C.

Sumer was a city-state in the southern part of Mesopotamia. A city-state consisted of a **sovereign** city and the surrounding area. It was like a small nation. The city-states of Ur, Eridu, and Uruk were Sumerian settlements.

Map of the ancient Near East showing the Fertile Crescent area, the birthplace of civilization

Each state was ruled by a priest-king. The king was a divine monarch who was treated as a god.

The kings established organized legal and political systems. Sumerian laws were considered to be inspired by the gods. Breaking a law was a crime against both the state and the gods.

Sumerian rulers performed religious ceremonies and judged disputes. They also led the military and directed trade. They ruled with the help of other priests. These priests surveyed land and assigned fields. They also distributed crops after a harvest.

The Sumerians had a **caste system**. The upper class included kings, priests, and nobles. Government officials and the wealthy also were considered upper class. The middle class included farmers, merchants, tradespeople, and soldiers. The lower class was made up of slaves.

Sumerian Law

One of the most important accomplishments of the Sumerians was the development of a legal system. Their law was one of the first to be recorded.

Sumerian law was designed to solve disputes. Justice fell somewhere between individual **revenge** and state-administered revenge. Victims had to take the accused to court. The court then listened to both sides, made a decision, and set the punishment for the crime. Often the victim or the victim's family had to carry out the sentence.

The laws were made to fit within the class system. Harming a priest or noble was a serious crime. Harming a slave or poor person was not as serious. But punishments for nobles were usually harsher than for someone from a lower class who committed the same crime.

Later, the Babylonians and the Assyrians based their laws on those of the Sumerians. The Sumerian legal system also influenced laws set down by the Hebrews.

Around 2000 B.C., a nearby tribe from Akkad conquered Sumer. Akkad united all of Mesopotamia under its rule.

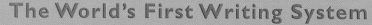

Early Sumerian states governed large areas. They needed a means to keep records. Over time, they developed an efficient system of writing. They used a form of shorthand made of wedged lines. They created this new writing by bending a reed against wet clay. Then they moved the reed back and forth one time. This form of writing was cuneiform, or wedge-shaped.

Cuneiform was the first written language, developed in about 3300 B.C. It had about 500 wedge-shaped characters. It lasted longer than any other form of writing except Chinese.

Sumerian Accomplishments

Calendars divided into 12 months were invented by the Sumerians. They based their calendars on the cycle of the moon. This led them to study astronomy.

The Sumerians also invented the wheel around 3400 B.C. The wheel was first used to make pottery. Later, it was used for transportation.

THE BABYLONIANS

The Babylonians lived along the Euphrates River. Their kings were considered gods, or divine monarchs. They built elaborate temples to their gods and goddesses. Many of their kings ruled as **despots**.

In around 2000 B.C., the Babylonians conquered Akkad. All of Sumer and Akkad were joined with the Babylonian kingdom.

Hammurabi and the Code of Laws

Hammurabi was a Babylonian king who ruled for 42 years (1792–1750 B.C.). He created the Code of Laws.

These laws were based on Sumerian law. Hammurabi's laws protected the weak from being **tormented** by the strong. But the laws were harsh. They demanded that the punishment fit the crime. An example of Hammurabi's laws was "an eye for an eye." Often different social classes received different treatments under the laws.

The Code of Laws consisted of 282 laws. The code addressed issues such as business and family relations, labor disputes, private property, and personal injury. These are a few examples of the laws.

- **Law 3:** If anyone brings an accusation of any crime before the elders and does not prove what he has charged, he shall, if it be a capital offense charged, be put to death.

- **Law 24:** If fire breaks out in a house, and someone who comes to put it out . . . takes the property of the master of the house, he shall be thrown into that self-same fire.

- **Law 121:** If anyone stores corn in another man's house, he shall pay him storage at the rate of one gur for every five ka of corn per year.

- **Law 195:** If a son strikes his father, his hands shall be **hewn** off.

- **Law 221:** If a physician heals the broken bone . . . of a man, the patient shall pay the physician five shekels in money.

After Hammurabi's death in 1750 B.C., Babylon was invaded. But the kingdom later reorganized. The Assyrians finally conquered Babylon in 689 B.C.

Hammurabi before the sun god (from the stele on which the Code of Laws was written)

Hammurabi's Code of Laws

In the winter of 1901–1902, a French archaeological team was working in what is today Shush, Iran. They found the eight-foot-high **stele** on which Hammurabi's laws had been written in cuneiform. It had been broken into three pieces.

The pieces were returned to Paris, France, where they were restored. The stele is now on display in the Louvre, a famous Paris museum.

THE PERSIANS

Around 2000 B.C., the Persians migrated to the Fertile Crescent from central Asia. They settled in a region east of the Fertile Crescent in present-day Iran. The Persians were warriors who rode horseback.

The Persian government was a monarchy ruled by kings. The Persians were religious people who worshiped many gods and goddesses. They prayed three times a day.

Cyrus the Great expanded the Persian Empire. He conquered Asia Minor and the Fertile Crescent. He was the first king of ancient times to feel it was his *duty* to conquer the world.

Eventually, the Persian Empire stretched all the way to India. Because the empire became so large, it was divided into 20 provinces. At its height, the Persian Empire included 40 million people.

From 549 B.C. to 331 B.C., the empire was divided into provinces, or satrapies. Each was governed by an official called a *satrap*. But the king of all Persia was still the final and absolute authority.

Hand-colored woodcut of the bas-relief of Cyrus the Great found in Pasargade, the capital of Persia

The satraps were responsible for collecting taxes and transferring them to the king's royal treasury. They also provided men for the royal army.

The king set up a secret service to serve as his eyes and ears. Members informed the king of affairs throughout the empire.

Around 330 B.C., the Persian Empire was conquered by the Greeks, and eventually, the Romans conquered the area.

Hittite statues of a warrior, art gods, and king

THE HITTITES

By 1600 B.C., the Hittites controlled Mesopotamia. Their empire stretched from Mesopotamia to Palestine. Their government was a monarchy, and they were ruled by a king. The Hittites were warriors known for their cruelty.

Archaeologists have discovered nearly 10,000 Hittite tablets. They were found in the ruins of Hattusa, which was located near the present-day Turkish town of Boghaz in Asia.

Some tablets were written in the Akkadian language. Others were written in the early Hittite language, which originated with the Indo-Europeans. Indo-Europeans lived in southern Russia around 2500 B.C. Still other tablets were written in cuneiform or hieroglyphics.

Art carving of a Hittite chariot running over a man

Most of the tablets contained decrees and laws. The Hittite laws were not as harsh as those of the Babylonians. And the Hittites were less concerned about maintaining a strict, controlling central government.

The Hittites even changed the role of the monarch. Monarchs in past civilizations had owned only their personal property. The Hittites gave their king ownership of all land over which he reigned. Citizens could control land under his ownership only if they were in the king's army.

The Hittite Empire was conquered around 1350 B.C. by the Assyrians.

THE ASSYRIANS

In 1350 B.C., the Assyrians lived in the same area formerly occupied by the Sumerians and Hittites. They settled in the cities of Ashur and Nineveh. Nineveh became the Assyrian capital.

Monarchs ruled the Assyrians for about 560 years. The Assyrians were merchants and fierce warriors. They often murdered their prisoners or made them slaves. They forced some captives into exile.

The main focus of the monarchy in Assyria was to build an empire, which it did. By 859 B.C., the Assyrian Empire included Syria, Lebanon, Palestine, and Lower Egypt. The height of the empire came when the Assyrians conquered the Babylonians in 745 B.C.

The upper class was made up of land-owning military leaders. Much of their wealth came from the **spoils** of their victories.

The Assyrian Empire lasted more than 700 years. It was conquered by the Babylonians. The Medes, people from what today is known as Iran, helped the Babylonians defeat Assyria around 612 B.C.

Hand-colored woodcut of soldiers using a battering ram during the siege of a city

Assyrian Accomplishments

Ashurbanipal was the last great king of Assyria. He assembled the first known library. His "books" were written on clay tablets in Sumerian cuneiform. About 30,000 fire-hardened tablets remain today. They provide much information about Mesopotamian civilizations.

THE HEBREWS

The Hebrews were nomads who lived in Canaan. Canaan was located between the Mediterranean Sea and the Jordan River. A drought forced the Hebrews into Egypt where the Egyptians made them slaves.

In around 1250 B.C., Moses became the Hebrew leader. He led the Hebrews out of Egypt. They wandered in the desert for 40 years until they finally returned to Canaan.

While in Canaan, each of the Twelve Tribes of Israel ruled itself. During this period, there was no central government. But certain individuals known as judges seemed to have control over the tribes. The judges often settled disputes between tribes. They also were military leaders. They organized members from all tribes into one army to battle foreigners who threatened to conquer them. The most important judge of this period was a woman named Deborah.

Twelve Tribes of Israel

According to Hebrew history, the Hebrews were organized into groups that could trace their ancestors back to one of the 12 sons of Jacob. Jacob was the son of Isaac, grandson of the first Hebrew, Abraham. These groups became known as the Twelve Tribes of Israel.

Moses reciting the Ten Commandments to the people

After about 200 years, the tribes united under one king. The Hebrew monarchs did not rule by divine right even though they worshiped one all-powerful God, Yahweh.

They built elaborate temples and palaces. They recorded their history and laws in the Old Testament of the Bible.

Around 586 B.C., Nebuchadnezzar II of Babylon conquered the Hebrews and took them captive.

THE PHOENICIANS

The Phoenicians lived on a narrow strip of land along the Mediterranean coast. This area is part of present-day Lebanon, Syria, and Israel. The Phoenician civilization flourished from around 1200 B.C. to 800 B.C.

The Phoenician city-states were individual kingdoms. The cities were **aristocracies** ruled by kings. Tyre, Sidon, and Biblos were three of the most important city-state kingdoms.

In the 800s B.C., councils of elders were established in each city-state. The elders were to keep the kings from using too much power. Some councils even had more power than the kings. Later, most cities were ruled by officials called *shofets*.

Around 1800 B.C., Phoenicia was invaded by the Egyptians. The Egyptians controlled the Phoenicians until 1400 B.C.

Phoenician Accomplishments

The Phoenicians became superb traders. They were skilled shipbuilders and excellent sailors. While under Persian rule, the Phoenicians furnished all the ships for the Persians when they attacked Greece during the Persian Wars.

The Phoenicians also were explorers. They were some of the first people to navigate at night by using the stars. They sailed across the Mediterranean Sea and built colonies in North Africa. The Phoenicians controlled trade within the Mediterranean area for 300 years.

The Phoenicians needed a way to keep track of their trading, so they developed an alphabet. Later, the Greeks added vowels and adapted it for their language. In many ways, the Phoenicians shaped the English alphabet.

During the 9th century B.C., the Assyrians conquered the
Phoenicians. The Assyrians ruled them until 612 B.C. Later,
Phoenicia became part of the Persian Empire. In 64 B.C., the
Romans conquered all of Phoenicia.

CHAPTER 2

The Nile Valley

EGYPT

The ancient Egyptian civilizations began along the Nile River. This region was in northeast Africa, where Africa and Asia meet. Ancient Egyptian civilizations lasted from around 3000 B.C. to 332 B.C.

The Egyptians had a form of government that was both a monarchy and a theocracy. Their kings (and several queens) were called *pharaohs*. They were considered gods. Dynasties of the Egyptian pharaohs ruled by "divine right." The Egyptians believed that the pharaoh was the god Horus in human form.

The ancient Egyptians formed the world's first central government. The 42 provinces of Egypt were divided into nomes. Nomarchs governed each province. The highest central-government official was called a *vizier*, who was responsible to only the pharaoh.

Pyramids at Giza

Painting from the tomb of Nakht, who was a trained sky watcher. He reported information about the stars to the pharaoh, Thutmose II.

Egyptian Accomplishments

The Egyptians developed one of the first religions to believe in life after death. They built huge pyramids (tombs) to preserve their **mummified** pharaohs. Some pyramids had many, many rooms. The Egyptians filled the pyramids with food, clothing, and jewelry that would be needed in the next life.

Egyptians were extraordinary engineers. They built huge temples and palaces. They also built irrigation ditches and canals.

The Egyptians invented their own form of writing. Their writing system consisted of elaborate symbols called *hieroglyphics*. They also invented papyrus, a paperlike material made from the stems of reeds. They recorded their own written history.

A basic form of arithmetic and a 365-day calendar were also Egyptian developments.

The Egyptians expanded their boundaries far beyond the Nile Valley. In the 1400s B.C., the Egyptians ruled Syria, Lebanon, and Palestine.

By the 1200s and 1100s B.C., the Egyptian kingdom had weakened. After 1000 B.C., power struggles were frequent among Egyptian dynasties. That led to the further decline of Egyptian civilizations.

During this time, Egypt was often under the control of non-Egyptians. These included the Assyrians and Persians. Alexander the Great added Egypt to his empire in 332 B.C.

Ptolemy I became the king of Egypt in 305 B.C. He began a dynasty that ruled until the Romans conquered Egypt in 30 B.C.

Cleopatra VII was born in 69 B.C. The name Cleopatra meant "glory of her family." She became queen at the age of 18. After Rome conquered Egypt, Cleopatra became known as Egypt's "Last Pharaoh."

Hindu goddess

THE GUPTA DYNASTY

The Gupta dynasty came to power in northern India around 320 A.D. This dynasty ruled for around 200 years. The Gupta period became known as the "Golden Age of India." The Gupta emperors were Hindus, but Buddhism also existed under Gupta rule.

Hinduism

Hinduism developed around 1500 B.C. Hinduism used the Sanskrit language. Hindus had thousands of gods and goddesses. Their priests memorized and sang long hymns.

The Hindus had a caste system similar to that of Buddhism. One exception was that Hindu priests also were called Brahmans. Another was that people excluded from the four castes were called *untouchables*. The untouchables were considered the lowest group of all.

Many people had trouble understanding the complex teachings of Hinduism. Traveling teachers helped to explain Hinduism by telling parables, which are short, simple stories intended to illustrate a moral or religious lesson.

Resurrection Buddha
Buddhism accepted the Hindu idea
that death leads to further rebirth.

Although the emperors ruled the empire, only the Ganges Valley was under their direct control. Much of the rest of the empire was allowed some independence as long as **tributes** were paid to the emperors.

The Guptas fell to the Huns in the early 500s A.D.

Gupta Accomplishments

Literature, sculpture, and other arts reached peaks never attained again in India.

CHAPTER 4

The Huang He Valley

Great Wall of China

The Chinese civilization developed along two rivers. One civilization was along the Huang He, which means "Yellow River." The other developed along the Chang Jiang, or "Long River." This region was in the southern part of present-day China.

THE HSIA DYNASTY

From around 1766 B.C., China was ruled by dynasties. The Hsia dynasty developed around 2000 B.C. It lasted until 1500 B.C. Although archaeologists have found little proof of this civilization, Chinese historians believe the dynasty was founded by Yu, a Chinese cultural hero.

THE SHANG DYNASTY

China's first documented dynasty, the Shang dynasty, began around 1500 B.C. The Shang ruled for about five centuries. They were the first to leave written records.

A priest-king ruled the city-states of the Shang. Two classes of people existed—commoners and nobles.

The people worshiped their ancestors and had many gods. Their religion lasted for thousands of years. They built elaborate tombs for their kings. Archaeologists also have found ruins of palaces and temples.

When a Shang king died, his next oldest brother inherited power. If there were no brothers, the oldest maternal nephew became king.

The Shang kingdom expanded its territory to include land between Mongolia and the Pacific Ocean.

Bronze wine vessel from the Shang Dynasty

Shang Accomplishments

The Shang invented a lunar calendar with 12 months of 30 days each. Their system of writing had more than 3,000 symbols. They wrote on turtle shells and pieces of bone. Today's Chinese writing evolved from the Shang writing system.

THE CHOU DYNASTY

The Chou (or Zhou) were nomads who lived west of the Shang. They invaded the Shang in around 1122 B.C. They ruled China until around 253 B.C.

Chou kings introduced the idea that they had been appointed to rule by heaven. This system of ruling by divine right was called Mandate of Heaven. Later, all Chinese dynasties adopted this theory.

The Chou created an early type of feudal system in China. Their system was a sophisticated type of tribal organization. The emperors appointed lords to divide land into small family units for peasant farmers. The peasant farmers pledged loyalty to the lords. The lords pledged loyalty to the emperors. This system depended more on family ties than later feudal systems did.

Around 256 B.C., the Chou were forced to move eastward. For the next several hundred years, China consisted of semi-independent states. The states constantly fought for control of all of China. This was known as the Age of Warring States.

Hand-colored woodcut of Confucius

Confucius

The great philosopher Confucius lived from around 551 B.C. to 497 B.C. His philosophy, Confucianism, stressed high moral standards. He wanted to improve society and promote a government that could better take care of the welfare of the people. Confucius traveled throughout China to spread his ideas.

Chou Accomplishments

The Chou learned how to remove iron from rocks. They then created powerful iron weapons. They built irrigation systems and roads. They built huge walls around their cities for protection.

THE CH'IN DYNASTY

In 221 B.C., the Ch'in dynasty defeated all of its rivals. It became the first Chinese empire with one central government. The word *China* comes from the name of this dynasty.

The Ch'in rulers gave peasant farmers the land they lived on. That ended the feudal system of government in China.

The last Ch'in emperor, Shih Huang-ti, was harsh and cruel. Civil war broke out and the Han defeated the Ch'in.

THE HAN DYNASTY

In 202 B.C., the Han dynasty gained control of China. Life improved under the Han emperors. Confucianism became the basis of Chinese government. Aristocrats held most of the important state offices. But securing a government position now depended on a person's qualifications instead of family ties and friendships.

Ch'in Accomplishments

The Ch'in dynasty (also called the Qin dynasty) lasted only 15 years—until around 206 B.C. But in that short time, the emperors standardized the Chinese writing system. They regulated weights and measures and built irrigation systems. They also began building the Great Wall of China to keep out **barbarian** invaders.

The Han dynasty expanded into present-day Tibet. The Hans also conquered present-day Korea. China became the greatest power in all of Asia.

Fighting among leaders of the Han dynasty led to its collapse. Around 200 A.D., China again divided into independent warring states. The states were rivals for the following 400 years.

詔儒講経

Emperor Sinen-Li of the Han dynasty
with scholars translating classical texts

Han Accomplishments

Astronomers charted the stars, water clocks and water pumps were invented, and silk looms were used. By 105 A.D., the Chinese had invented paper.

Education became important and a central university was established. Styles in poetry and prose were developed that are still used in Chinese literature today.

CHAPTER 5

Japan

Historians believe people have lived in present-day Japan since 8000 B.C. But little is known about them.

The territory of Japan once was attached to mainland Asia. In time, Japan became a chain of volcanic islands. Today, Japan consists of four big islands and thousands of **islets**. They begin off the coast of Siberia in the north. They run down to Formosa in the south. The Japanese **archipelago** is more than 2,500 miles long.

Japanese wall painting

Today, people of Japan plant rice just as their ancestors did thousands of years ago.

THE JOMON

The early people of Japan were called Jomon. Their clans lived in villages where they hunted and fished. They probably were governed by a tribal chief, or king, who was also the priest.

Between 1000 B.C. and 500 B.C., the Jomon began to plant rice. This led to the beginning of agriculture and a more permanent lifestyle.

The first recorded contact between Japan and China was in 57 A.D. A Japanese king from Wo, the Chinese name for Japan, met with a Chinese emperor.

Around 200 A.D., the Yamato from Korea invaded Japan.

THE YAMATO

The Yamato ruled from 250 A.D. until 710 A.D., after the ancient period. The Yamato spread Chinese and Korean culture in Japan.

During this period, Japan was ruled by an emperor. The current royal family of Japan can trace its ancestors to the Yamato emperors.

The Chinese had a major influence on Japan. The Yamato adopted the Chinese form of government as well as their religion and writing style.

Europe

THE GREEKS

Ancient Greece was located on a peninsula in southeastern Europe bordering the Mediterranean Sea. The land was mountainous and the city-states were separated from one another.

Greece included about 200 independent city-states. Each city-state, many of which were on the numerous islands of Greece, was called a *polis*. City-states developed their own independent governments. The most popular city-states were Athens and Sparta.

Early Greeks were ruled by tyrants and aristocrats. They also were ruled by monarchies with kings.

The Greeks worshiped many gods and goddesses. Each god or goddess was considered a ruler of some part of nature. The Greeks invented myths, or stories, about the gods. They believed that their gods and goddesses lived on Mount Olympus. The Olympic Festival was held every four years in honor of the Greek god Zeus.

Temple of Apollo at Delphi

The Olympic Games: 776 B.C.–394 A.D.

The Greeks idolized physical fitness and athletics. They built gymnasiums and stadiums for enhancing and testing physical skills.

The most famous of their many athletic games were the Olympics that began in 776 B.C. Men and boys traveled from all over Greece to participate in the Olympic Games.

Winners received a wreath of olive leaves from a sacred tree near the Temple of Zeus. There were no second or third place winners.

Olympic winners were treated as heroes. Later, they often became politicians or trainers. Some winners even received pensions from their city-states.

Today, the Olympics take place every two years, and athletes from all over the world participate.

Zeus, king of the Greek gods and god of the sky and weather

The World's First Democracy

Around 570 B.C., Cleisthenes was born to a noble family in Athens. When Cleisthenes was ten years old, his brother-in-law seized power. He ruled as a tyrant. Yet his reign was remembered as the "Golden Age" of Athens. His son, Hippias, became the next ruler of Athens. He became an increasingly brutal **dictator**.

In 514 B.C., Cleisthenes asked Sparta for help in overthrowing Hippias. By 510 B.C., Athens was **liberated** from tyrants. Cleisthenes was in his 60s. Because he had helped defeat Hippias, he hoped to rule Athens.

Another nobleman, Isagoras, challenged Cleisthenes' power. Cleisthenes appealed to the commoners and promised sweeping **reforms**. But in 508 B.C., the aristocrats helped Isagoras gain power.

In 507 B.C., the commoners of Athens revolted against Isagoras. They banished the tyrant and seized power for themselves.

The commoners recalled Cleisthenes, who was in **exile**. They asked him to form a new government that included commoners. Cleisthenes created a government that we now know as a democracy.

The name *democracy* comes from the Greek word *demos* that means "people" and the Greek word *kratein* that means "to rule."

The democracy of Cleisthenes included both aristocrats and commoners. This was the first government of any ancient civilization to do so.

Cleisthenes formed a general assembly of all free men. The men would meet and discuss issues of running the government. Each man had one vote. This is known as a direct democracy.

In 507 B.C., this democracy became the world's first government ruled by many people. By the 4th century B.C., there were hundreds of Greek democracies. But the most stable democracy was that of Athens. Other city-states still had oligarchies and monarchies.

The Romans conquered Greece in 146 B.C.

Alexander the Great

In 338 B.C., Philip II of Macedonia conquered all of Greece and united the Greek city-states. Macedonia was a northern Greek province. Philip II was murdered in 335 B.C.

Alexander, the son of Philip II, set out to conquer the world. Alexander the Great then built the largest empire the world had known—stretching over one million square miles. His conquests included the Persian Empire, Egypt, and western India. He also conquered countries that are now present-day Pakistan and Afghanistan.

Alexander the Great continued to expand his empire for ten more years. In 324 B.C., he died of exhaustion and a fever at the age of 32. Through his conquests, Alexander the Great spread Greek culture to Asia and the Indus Valley.

Parthenon ruins at the site of the city-state of Athens

Greek Accomplishments

Hippocrates (460 B.C.–377 B.C.) was a Greek doctor who founded scientific medicine. He thought the practice of medicine should be based on observation. Present-day doctors still take the Hippocratic Oath when they begin to practice medicine. The oath describes medical ethics based on the ideas of Hippocrates.

The Greeks made ageless contributions to literature and theater. Homer, the first Greek poet, wrote the *Iliad* and the *Odyssey*.

The Greeks created stunning architecture, pottery, sculpture, and paintings. Greek architecture is still influential today.

The Greek scholar Archimedes made brilliant mathematical discoveries.

Greek pottery

THE ROMANS

Rome was a region in present-day Italy. There were three periods in Roman history—the monarchy, the republic, and the empire. In 509 B.C., the people of Rome revolted against their monarch and declared Rome a republic.

The Roman Republic

The republican form of government was similar to, yet different from, the Greek democracy. It was similar in that the common people gained the right to vote along with aristocrats. In Greece, the male citizens voted directly on issues. In the republican government of Rome, male citizens did not vote directly. The plebeians, or common people, elected representatives to vote for them. The Roman Republic also had a written code of laws to limit the power of the wealthy class of **patricians**.

The Roman Empire

During the republic, Rome continued to expand its borders. Rome maintained a huge army that lived in the conquered territories when they were not at battle. Continual warfare created influential generals, many of whom were hungry for political power.

In 51 B.C., Julius Caesar and his huge army conquered Gaul, which is modern-day France. He then returned to Rome. He declared himself dictator of the Roman world. Caesar was murdered in 44 B.C.

In 31 B.C., Caesar's adopted son, Octavian, declared himself emperor. He took the title of "Augustus" and became the first true emperor of Rome.

Augustus extended the Roman Empire. He introduced a period of peace and stability that lasted for around 200 years.

During the 5th century A.D., the Romans found it difficult to defend their vast frontiers. Barbarian invaders constantly challenged the Roman Empire. In 410 A.D., the Visigoths sacked Rome. In 476 A.D., the Roman Empire was invaded and the last Roman emperor abdicated, or resigned. The fall of the Roman Empire in 476 A.D. marked the end of the ancient period of history.

Hand-colored engraving of the Roman emperor Augustus

CHAPTER 7

The Americas

Other ancient civilizations developed around the same time as those in Mesopotamia, Asia, and Europe. Many of these civilizations were in the Western Hemisphere. Canada and the United States are part of the Western Hemisphere, as are Mexico, Central America, and South America.

The first advanced civilization in the Western Hemisphere began in present-day Mexico and Central America. This region is called Mesoamerica. It also includes the western coast of South America.

THE OLMECS

The Olmec civilization began along the Gulf Coast of southern Mexico. This civilization thrived around 400 A.D. Priest-emperors, for whom the people built large temples, ruled.

Archaeologists have uncovered impressive works of art by the Olmec people. Some of these are huge carved heads made from stone and masks and statuettes of jade. The Olmecs also created a calendar and a system of hieroglyphics.

Around 300 A.D., the Olmecs vanished. Archaeologists believe that much of their culture was absorbed by other invading people of the time.

Olmec head sculpture

THE CHAVIN

The Chavin lived in and around the Andes Mountains of northern Peru. Emperor-priests ruled the Chavin. The Chavin built a pilgrimage center at Chavin de Huantar. This coastal settlement flourished for around 700 years.

The Chavin who lived in the mountains chewed coca, from which cocaine is **extracted**. Coca was used for holy **rites** and to cope with the cold climate.

These people were noted for their fine gold work and pottery. Archaeologists also found ruins of elaborate stone carvings.

The Chavin civilization disappeared around 200 B.C.

THE MAYA

The Maya civilization began about 250 A.D.—near the end of the ancient period of history. It flourished far beyond the ancient period. The Spanish conquered the Maya in the 1500s A.D.

The Maya lived over a huge area of land. Their territory included present-day Honduras, El Salvador, and Guatemala. It also included Belize and the entire Yucatán Peninsula of Mexico. Their empire reached from the Pacific coast to the coasts along the Gulf of Mexico. The territory also included jungles and 33 volcanoes.

Mayan temple in Belize

The Maya civilization was the most advanced Mesoamerican civilization. Each city had a strong central government that governed its surrounding area. Some large cities each controlled one or more smaller cities. Each city had a ruler who usually was succeeded by his younger brother or by his son. In some cases, a single family ruled for hundreds of years. Priests were the supreme rulers. They ran the governments and ruled many cities. Priests were considered to have supernatural powers that gave them the divine right to rule.

Mayan Accomplishments

The Maya were excellent architects and engineers. They built towering temples and stepped pyramids in the jungles.

Mayan works of art were detailed and impressive. The Maya developed a complex hieroglyphic system of writing that was much like Egyptian hieroglyphics. They wrote on 20-foot-long sheets of tree bark. They folded each sheet into pleats like an accordion.

The Maya developed a 365-day calendar. Their number system was very similar to most modern number systems. They were the first people to develop the concept of zero.

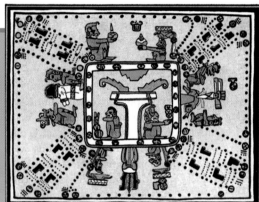

Mayan calendar

NORTH AMERICA CIVILIZATIONS

Native Americans have lived in North America since around 9000 B.C. Many of these early peoples lived in what is now southeastern Canada. Some lived in what is now the United States, east of the Mississippi River.

These people were hunters and gatherers who probably lived in clans. Later, chieftains governed them. Shamans, or priests with "supernatural powers," also were important.

North American cultures were much earlier than those in Mesoamerica. Archaeologists have not found evidence of centralized forms of government in North America.

The Adena

The Adena lived in Ohio, Indiana, Kentucky, and West Virginia from about 500 B.C. to 100 B.C. They raised crops and made excellent pottery. Their form of government was a monarchy.

Archeologists have found the tombs of the Adena's rulers and important people. The tombs were covered with large mounds of earth. The Adena have been named the Mound Builders.

The remains found show that the Adena were very large people. Both men and women usually were over six feet tall with powerful builds. They were buried in log tombs under the mounds.

Siltstone smoking pipes were found under the mounds. They are great examples of prehistoric Indian art.

The Hopewell

The Hopewell lived in present-day southern Ohio, Illinois, along the Mississippi River Valley, and in Missouri from 200 B.C. to 400 A.D. Resources were abundant in these areas.

The Hopewell are thought to be descendants of the Adena. Their cultures seemed to overlap. The Hopewell leaders were not powerful kings who commanded armies of slaves and soldiers. People from many villages worked together to build mounds for their dead rulers and important people.

Hopewell Mound, Mound City National Historic Site, Ohio

Anasazi cliff palace

Many artifacts have been found under their mounds. Tools found included sheet copper, knives, and hooks. Pottery has also been found.

The Anasazi

The Anasazi began living in present-day New Mexico, Arizona, Utah, and Colorado around 200 A.D. Their climate was very dry with little rain to grow crops. They built canals as irrigation systems to collect rainwater for their fields.

The Anasazi also built large apartmentlike houses into the sides of cliffs. They left their villages around 1200 A.D., probably because of a severe drought.

The Anasazi were the ancestors of the present-day Pueblo Nation. The Pueblo Nation includes the Acoma, Zuni, and Hopi Nations.

Conclusion

Ancient civilizations came and went, and their forms of government went with them. The earliest rulers were chieftains who ruled clans. Chieftains had absolute power and were early forms of monarchs.

Monarchies became a popular form of government. Many civilizations also had priest-kings or priest-queens who ruled by divine right. These governments were both monarchies and theocracies.

Ancient China had a feudal system during the Chou dynasty. The feudal system was a type of tribal organization. This early form of feudalism was further developed during the Middle Ages.

In early Greece, one powerful aristocrat ran the country. These tyrants were monarchs with absolute power. Greece also had oligarchies where few ruled.

In the 700s B.C., a Greek aristocrat, Cleisthenes, invented a democracy as a form of government. This government included both aristocrats and common people for the first time in history. Democracy was, and is, a government ruled by many.

Around this same time, the first republic was developed in Rome. In a republic, people elect others to represent them or to vote for them. Neither the first democracy nor the first republican form of government lasted for long.

The Acropolis, Athens, Greece

Greek philosopher Aristotle (384–322 B.C.) claimed that "good governments best serve the people." He also said "bad governments best serve the man in power."

Aristotle's system of classifying governments was used for centuries. Some ancient governments were good. More of them were bad. Few of them best served all the people.

Some of these ancient forms of government are still present today. Monarchs, dictators, and emperors still rule countries. But few of them have the absolute power of ancient rulers.

Feudalism and oligarchies are not among modern governments. But tyrannies still exist in some countries.

Aristotle

Socialism and communism, newer forms of governments, are present today. Both forms focus on government ownership of everything shared by everyone. And various forms of democracies are still popular and thriving.

Colosseum, Rome, Italy

Internet Connections

http://www.wsu.edu:8080/~dee

You're invited to browse through the dust and heat of one of the first cultures. Tour the mysteries of ancient civilizations and their governments.

http://www.mrdowling.com/index.html

Journey through the ancient lands of Mesopotamia, Egypt, China, Japan, Greece, Rome, and the Americas to learn about the civilizations that lived there.

http://www.historyforkids.org

This Web site is loaded with information about Egypt, Mesopotamia, Greece, and Rome.

http://www.encyclopedia.com

Search this kid-friendly encyclopedia for topics relating to ancient governments. Then click on the many links to further your knowledge.

Pyramid of Khefren at Giza in Egypt

Glossary

absolute having total power and authority

archaeologist scientist who studies ancient cultures by examining remains of buildings, graves, tools, and other artifacts (see separate entry) usually dug up from the ground

archipelago group or chain of islands

aristocracy government of a country ruled by a small group of people, especially related nobles

aristocrat member of the highest social class in a country

artifact object, such as a tool or ornament, made by a human being that tells something about a culture

barbarian member of a people whose culture and behavior was considered uncivilized, especially in ancient times

caste system any organized manner that divides people into classes according to their rank, wealth, or profession

city-state independent state consisting of a sovereign (see separate entry) city and its surrounding territory

despot ruler with absolute (see separate entry) powers

dictator leader who rules a country with absolute (see separate entry) power, usually with force

exile unwilling absence from one's own country, usually enforced by a government or court as a punishment

extracted obtained something from a source, usually by separating it from the other material

feudal relating to a legal social system in which commoners held land from lords in exchange for services

general assembly highest governing body made up of citizens or their representatives

hewn past tense of *hew*; to cut off with a sharp tool, usually an ax

islet small island

liberated released an individual, group, population, or country from political or military control

mummified relating to the act of preserving the body of a dead person for burial

nomad person who wanders from place to place in search food and water

patrician member of an aristocratic family of ancient Rome whose privileges included the exclusive right to hold certain offices

prehistoric relating to the period before history was first recorded in writing

reform change or improvement, especially social or political

revenge something done to get even with someone else who has caused harm

rite solemn and ceremonial act that follows the rule customary to a community, especially a religious group

seal ring or stamp with a raised or engraved symbol or emblem

sovereign self-governing and not ruled by any other state

spoils valuables or property seized by the victor in a conflict

stele ancient upright stone slab or pillar, usually engraved, inscribed, or painted

tormented caused someone pain, torture, or hardship

tribute payment made by one ruler of state to another as a sign of submission

Index